Back Door Area

The critics have spoken...

"Laframboise does an excellent job of translating the rhythm and feel of the typical murder mystery into the realities of a snail's eye view. The story is clever and effectively conveys the point of view of the snails and the various limitations and talents available to them."

-- Robert Turner, Tangent Online, 2017

«Michèle Laframboise impresses the hell out of me. She writes beautifully in more than one genre, more than one form, and more than one language.»

-- Kristine Kathryn Rusch, Fiction River, 2017

Michèle Laframboise

Back Door Area

A Case from the GGPD Files

Echofictions

Greater Garden Snail Police - 2

A WOW Story

Cover design by Echofictions
Cover pictures of snail © Shutterstock
Author portrait © Gilles Gagnon
Interior illustrations by the author

This book published by : Echofictions
Mississauga, Ontario

www.echofictions.com

ISBN 978-1-988339-73-3 (print)

Table of Contents

Dedication   vii

Back Door Area   1

Heartfelt Thanks   45

Accolades   46

About the Author   47

Other books by Michèle   49

Friends' List   51

Yearning for more Stories?   52

For Josette

who loves gardens,

cats and mysteries!

Back Door Area

1

LATE SPRING HAD blossomed with vivid flowers explo-
ding everywhere in Garden before seamlessly oozing
into early summer, with a white-hot sun that made any
mineral slab a torture to glide over.

Only the sturdiest officers would dare to slime over
a flat stone, spending precious moisture along the way.

Given the pounding heat, it was an unusual occur-
rence to meet the GGPD Chief above ground level.
His scarred shell brushed against the cabbage leaves
as he chatted with his high-ranking officers, discussing
the new recruits that were tested today.

The orange and violet patterns of the seven-cycle-old veteran snail had faded under hundreds of scars. It was said the Chief had always been large for his age group, and that even death claws avoided his shell.

Lots of conjectures circulated about the Chief, most false, all equally terrifying. Some thought he had unholy alliances with earthworms, others said he counted the current wasp nest's queen among his informers. (I doubted the last one was true: the queen never left the papery globe-shaped nest hanging under the gables over Back Door Area.)

The Chief wisely let the rumors float, strengthening up the ones encouraging loyalty.

Usually, he had his meals carried down his burrow where he could munch at it leisurely while conferring with his subordinates or listening to his informants. (The latter used a root-infested tunnel winding far away from the busy cabbage area.)

At midday, most sloggers kept to the shade, some retiring inside their spiraled shell to wait for sunset. Accordingly, crime was low.

It was a good time to gobble some lettuce without competition, even if evaporation gave their leaves a fibrous taste. I kept an eyestalk directed toward the knot of officers.

The Chief had planted himself under a leave, watching the ongoing action on the racetrack. Someone had pushed a tiny, pit-encrusted raspberry under his wide foot.

Of course, the Chief ignored the gift, his short stalks waving and sniffing the air, emitting a joke to the officers around him. But the way his mottled foot was oozing around the delicacy told me he had appreciated the present.

The yummy tiny strawberries so abundant in spring were getting scarce. It had become a competition between GGPD officers to get one of those delicacies to the Chief.

If you wanted him to forget minor mistakes or a low rate of crime-solving, strawberry-chasing was the way to go.

Not for me.

Despite being only three-cycle-old, my sense of smell was the most refined in all divisions, giving me the best crime-solving rate of the GGPD, a feat I did not mind sharing with my talented patrol partner.

I was too far to sniff what the Chief was talking about, probably some reminiscences of the famed Cabbage Wars that most of us hadn't lived through. New territories had been gained or bargained, and Garden had expanded into the Greater Garden jurisdiction.

The laugh emissions that followed were stained with an acid tang. Most officers hadn't caught the gist of the joke, but they were emulating (badly) an enthusiastic response.

An acrid signal drifted from the officers stationed at the perimeter of the racetrack. All stalks turned toward the flat stone rising from the granular soil of our vegetable patch.

The slab's height reached two slogger lengths up from the moist soil where we congregated. Forming a stark contrast to the hazy sky, the shells of police candidates were heaving up and down, hurrying after a bigger one along the edge.

Scents acrid, acid or sweet wafted from the crowd to encourage the racers. I smiled inwardly.

The green candidate officers had no hope to catch up to the leading racer, his scarred shell with the GGPD mark advancing at an astonishing rate. Zgouish was my partner, a four-cycle-old slogger who used his muscular body as a screen to hide his astuteness. He could have risen in the ranks of officers, but he preferred the physical exertions of field patrols to the humdrum of a plush underground office.

As he reached the scented finish line, his big shell tipping over the edge of the slab, an explosion of honeyed smells greeted his victory.

I sensed mischief from the smaller one behind Zgouish, stinging disappointment from the second contender, a lean fellow, while the third one behind exhaled tints of fear to be stuck in such an exposed place, his mismatched eyestalks waving this and that way. The fourth broadcast his fear all around. Clearly, he had been in some scuffle because a crack ran across his shell.

Fear of exposed places was healthy, of course, but the GGPD trained his officers to dispel instinctive reactions that could hinder their service.

At this time of day, the heat played in our favor. No predators would be darting from the sky to pounce upon unsuspecting Garden citizens. Most death claws observed the midday truce, none of them eager to waste precious energy and moisture by flapping their wings in the dry atmosphere.

The fifth candidate lagging on the track was clearly more intent on munching than slogging, a juicy grass blade protruding from his wide mouth. No wonder his shell was so big for a two-cycle-old!

I had thought all candidates accounted for when I noticed, way, *way* behind the other racers, three medium-sized spiraled shells advancing in such proximity that they were crowding each other. Not efficient.

Why couldn't those quarter-brains hurry on? If not for the midday truce, their awkward clustering would have made them food for the death claws' young. This pounding heat would suck them dry before they crossed the mucous end line...

I concentrated on finishing my meal, relieved that recruit-training fell to Zgouish.

2

I SLOGGED MY WAY toward the Chief, wondering if he had guessed the provenance of the raspberry. Most heavyset officers couldn't slime up a raspberry stem without bending the plant. My reduced size was an ally.

A heavy shell bumped against mine. Correction: my reduced size was also a problem.

The medical examiner, a hefty slogger, made his way without even saluting me. He planted his rank foot right in front of me, the swirls of his five-cycle shell hiding the Chief to my view.

I oozed around him.

Sensing my move, the ME lifted his head and twisted his earth-sucking foot suggestively, the edges rippling in a fast 4–8 cadence. Thankful for the open space, I turned away from him.

Since a freak accident had transformed me from hermo to egg-layer, several officers either snubbed me or tried, repeatedly, to mate on the job.

On this last topic, the ME's assistant had mimicked his boss fixation on me, doubling the annoyance of sliming alone in the narrow corridors outside the lab. I learned to keep a safe distance, or have my patrol partner close by.

The Chief tolerated me because my high crime-solving rate reflected well on the GGPD. Only my partner had shown genuine interest—and once, more than a purely professional interest—in me as a fellow police officer.

By now, Zgouish was oozing vertically down the slab, taking his sweet time, basking in the glorious odors emanating from his patrol colleagues.

The Chief emitted a faint recognition scent, waving his lone eyestalk. The Cabbage War had left traces on his heavy body, his seven-cycle shell almost discolored, one eyestalk missing, his foot muscles undulating as he raised his head, exposing a wavy lip from which a lone drop of red juice glistened.

The ring of subordinates crowding the chief was by now assessing the provenance of the tasty fruit he was happily digesting. I let them speculate: it was an enjoyable groveling moment.

Invariably, one of them would pretend he had climbed a raspberry plant to get the gift. I was painfully aware of the difficulties of climbing along those hairy stalks to get the sweet fruit. It was not my first offering to the Chief, but the first I had risked while his being outside.

Stealth was the name of the game, and I had become a master at it.

I expected the ME's horny assistant to brag about it, mentally preparing my witty rebuttal. It would be a sweet revenge for his unwelcome mating attempts. The tech was heavy and way out of shape. And that coward would never dare ascending a stem to get food.

(It was dangerous to rise over the grass blades, making oneself a juicy target for the winged predators. Fortunately, raspberry plants clung to each other in a tight and spiny embrace that I had learned to navigate.)

But the stupid ME assistant did not emit the tiniest whiff of pride. The bragging, this time, came from a new direction.

I heard a mushy shock as the closest contender, a two-cycle old, let himself fall from the edge of the slab, head and foot pulled inside his shell. The small slogger touched ground *before* Zgouish did. His shell rolled a short distance until inertia prevailed. He stuck out his glistening head and unrolled his long eyestalks, emitting a triumphant *I did it!*

The small, strongly scented slogger advanced almost under the Chief and sent a puff of fruity brag. His shell was so shiny that his fresh **GGPD** mark stood out in vivid contrast.

"Was it good? Those are quite hard to come by!"

Oooh, the arrogant little prick!

The candidate was small enough that his claim would not be challenged by any officers. And if I came along claiming the gift-taking, it would come across as the reaction of a frustrated egg sack.

Dung.

I drew a small consolation that the Chief's big foot was exuding a watery juice, his sides undulating in a slow pattern of annoyance.

The trio of slow sloggers paused while oozing down the vertical wall, sending clear olfactive signals to the braggart. The three of them wanted to … mate!

And, yes, the small show-off was releasing powerful "I-want-U" pheromones, to the officers' consternation (or excitement). Only the air moving away from me toward the sex-starved candidates prevented me from falling shell over foot into a mating frenzy.

The emissions were abruptly cut down by a stern command from the Chief. The steamy candidate vanished in the direction of Headquarters' entrance. The trio of slow sloggers was greeted with the same acidic scold and disappeared as fast.

The other contenders had already vanished under some cabbage leaves, except the big one, still munching a whitish root.

What a pathetic bunch! I hadn't even got their scent signatures.

Sloggers didn't get a name before they had managed to survive their first cycle. Police candidates were recruited on their second spring, their shell marked with the GGPD badge.

They were tested and trained through the summer. If they survived the training, a permanent mark would be etched on the main spire of their shell. The GGPD mark, an olfactive and visible badge, gave some protection. Besides, it did wonders for the morale of the candidates.

Some older officers had balked at the idea of marking candidates, but the Chief had floated the idea last fall, after a whole unmarked bunch of would-be officers had been lost to elements and predation before midsummer.

I had enrolled after a second call for candidates and passed the trials with a fair success, despite the black mark of my accidental sex change. I saw the GGPD as a refuge from my past. I would glide over a clean slate and forget I had ever been so stupid and light-footed.

For a time, the flurry of oozing this and that way in the office burrows, with scent calls crossing each other in the morning air had felt exciting. Of course, it hadn't stayed a liberating experience for long, as the opposition I quickly encountered shown me. The Medical examiner had taken to trap me in the narrow corridors. His stupid tech followed his pattern, and only judicious moves had spared me from mating on the job (a _no-no_ in the GGPD book).

Not long after I joined, I had been called to step in for a dead investigator. It had been a sealed-burrow murder case; the investigator was making progress but had been squashed down by a giant's foot before he could send his report. Despite the scents getting thinner, I took the case from the start and managed to solve it, meeting my present partner on the way.

I extended both eyestalks to get a good look at Zgouish's athletic body. He retracted his muscular foot from the wall and oozed his way toward the cluster of spectators under the cabbage leaf. My insides went all wobbly.

Zgouish had to be strong, of course, to carry that heavy, scarred shell of his. He often acted as a law enforcer and had been in countless situations requesting the use of physical force. That was why he had been tasked with racing the candidates over the slab.

Someone not well acquainted with the GGPD would see my partner as nothing more than a big bad-footed brute. I was among the few who knew about his special abilities and his keen mind, two things Zgouish didn't care to have publicized in the service.

His shell bore the mark of an old crack in the central spires, a dramatic event in his first cycle that saw his clutch-bros die in a beer trap in Back Door Area. (There was a reason why BDA was a forbidden zone. Only the stupid ants and flies ignored the scented warnings posted around the perimeter.)

As the ring of officers closed around him and the exuberant scents puffed in, I oozed back down the lettuce alley, sniffing tantalizing sprouts.

3

IT WAS A GOOD TIME to be alive in the Greater Garden jurisdiction.

The crime rate had dropped since the Basement Incident had swept off a bunch of low-life dealers, mid-spring.

It happened from time to time: those incredibly fast-moved giants stomping around their territory, squishing everything and everyone in their way. I had filled three reports about it, because the Basement Incident happened while I was investigating a dealer's murder.

My solving of the case should have reflected nicely on my career... if I had been your run-of-the-mill hermo.

But as a mere egg layer, my shining report gathered a curt nod from the Chief, critics from colleagues who would have preferred to ooze up and down the perp's shell, and feigned indifference from the ME. (Feigned, because I could pick up traces of formic acid from his emanations, belying his eyestalks signals. As I exited the Chief's office, the ME assistant had tried a mating attempt on me. His face met Zgouish's towering, oozing foot.)

I chased off those gloomy thoughts to concentrate on the moist underside of a lettuce leave. All in all, things were looking up, and no envious colleague could erase my success rate.

The addictive yeast-ball traffic would stop until a new generation of lowlifes sprang up. For a blessed while, we could concentrate on the usual Garden public security problems: trespassers in Back Door Area, depressive types slogging north to get run over by rolling blackdeaths in the Gray Canyon, the green snake depredations...

For the time being, the guards stationed on the perimeter of Back Door Area had reported no unlawful entrances and the summer's pounding heat discouraged the most down-on-their-luck sloggers to undertake the long trek to the Gray Canyon. As for the green snake, it hadn't moved since yesterday, its copper water-gushing head resting over coils of green plastic.

My main concern would be the brown balls of aster pods carried everywhere by the wind. That junk food's spicy scent erased most ambient smells (lovely on a crime scene investigation!)

A scent call carrying the unique signature of the Chief wafted to my receptor stalks.

The distance had diluted its strength, but the signal remained recognizable by someone endowed with an uncanny sense of smell. You never ignore a summoning by the GGPD chief. Maybe he had guessed the yummy raspberry's real provenance.

Fat wormy chance.

I knew from experience that he would never express his appreciation around his officers. If he did acknowledge the gift, he would rather scold me about the foolhardiness of climbing a high stem.

I gobbled up the rest of the soil-speckled leave and heaved my shell upright, then slogged to join the cluster of police officers.

A few dozens of heartbeats later, I was squeezing myself between two officers to get in visual and olfactive reach of the Chief. His giant discolored shell dominated the group.

I noticed then the candidates huddling together, the younger one's stalks questing warily about. A new set of pheromones floated around, laden with authority. I closed all my scent to lower my emissions.

When the only scents came from the blooming flowers and the greenery, the Chief spoke.

"Inspector Gowoon, you will take over the training of the new batch of candidates."

I distinctively felt the lettuce leaves boil in my stomach. He couldn't have meant it! No way I would ooze even a quarter-Garden width from this unwary and headstrong bunch! I calmed down and chose my pheromones wisely.

"With all due respect, Chief, I'm not the best officer for training the recruits."

For once, the ME approved my declaration, his head raising high, his creased skin emitting confirmation pheromones. His stupid goony assistant waved his shell left and right, his foot's edge undulating in a subdued mating dance. How I wished for a deathclaw to swoop down on him!

Of course, the Chief's attention at that moment was wholly directed at me. My hesitation didn't sit well with him. I raised my eyestalk firmly in his direction.

This kind of task would normally be carried on by a sturdy chap like Zgouish. I bent my left eye stalk in his direction. My partner's eye stalks barely moved, and his emissions were kept minimal, but his foot's edges were undulating in a two-four cadence, disclosing his own misgivings. He was as surprised as I was.

"My strengths lie with smelling out perps," I signed.

Candidate training could be a career trap. I wondered if the ME had puffed out this suggestion while I was away. Opening my receptive channels, I trained them on him, while my eyestalks remained at rigid attention, glistening with respectful pheromones. This was a learned ability, essential for surviving in the GGPD ranks since I got the coveted post of chief inspector.

"Gowoon," he signed, "No one can deny you have achieved the best crime-solving rate in Garden."

An agreeable basking sensation wove all over my foot, but I refrained from showing any excitement.

"However," the Chief signed, "it has come to my attention (a slight nod of his eyeless stalk to his left) that the candidates would get a more thorough education coming from the number one investigator in GGPD, instead of leaving them with some heavy muscle intent on putting his foot on the face of others."

This was a deliberate slight on Zgouish's less than stellar records, off service. His slugfests near the twin Composter Bins might have come to the Chief's attention, but I suspected the ME had the upper lip in ushering the scandalous news to the Chief's smell receptors.

No shocked scents came from my partner. Zgouish knew perfectly well how he was perceived by the rest of the GGPD officers, and he secretly worked to keep that reputation intact.

He responded with that bad-slogger shrug that I had come to relish. It was part of his charm, to be able to get away with such a move in front of the Chief.

Two hermo officers on the right of the Chief got busy cleaning their eye stalks, to avoid displaying any attraction.

I was no less shocked by the announcement, and angered.

Despite my efforts to keep my skin emanations to the lowest perception level, tiny beads of sweat formed on my upper lip, betraying my irritation. The ME's receptors picked up the salt content, and his fat foot undulated, a slow 1–2 cadenced wave of satisfaction, undistinguishable to the casual observer.

He couldn't prevent some of those happy pheromones puffing out, of course, but those could easily be interpreted as a general enthusiasm brought by the idea of new blood joining the GGPD.

"We have eight candidates," the Chief went on. "Which is a promising number."

Somehow, the scent accompanying his signed words told me that this batch would be composed of less-than-promising individuals.

Most of the officers were happy to avoid the exhausting task of training a bunch of new officers that "promised" to be a mouthful. Their released emotions were only matched by my own disappointment. A quick twist of my receptor stalks revealed the glee emanating from the ME, his foot dance unmistakable.

His devious plan congealed in my brain. I would be stuck with a stubborn, risk-loving, headstrong band, exhausted from spending too much command pheromones on them. They would wander off or die in the process, which would do wonders for my ratings. The survivors, if there were any, would be carted off to menial tasks, leaving the same circle of older officers on top of things for another season.

This was why Zgouish wasn't eager to join this sclerosed circle. I kept still, pondering my response.

Yes, I had better things to do, and the eggs maturing in my belly were a powerful reminder of the other way my fruitful career could ooze into sticky territory.

I *could* ask to supervise the aster pod-sweeping detachment. It was a necessary task to clear the precinct burrow off those pests, but this was a low-end job carried by the least talented in the GGPD. That stint would stain my record.

Moreover, there was no assurance of getting back my enviable investigator post after I had laid my eggs in a discreet and safe place. The horrid spicy, junk-food scent of the pods would play havoc with my sense of smell. I was afraid it would lower my crime-solving rate afterward.

Keeping my pneumostome aperture clean was the main reason I refrained from yeast-induced and strong-smelled excitation (barring one notable exception). I also absorbed lots of moisture through my skin, to keep my receptors fresh. So, no pod-sweeping duty for me.

As for lab work inside the GGPD burrow with the snobbish ME and his horny assistant?

No.

Sucking.

Way.

After two heartbeats, I lowered my four stalks, the longer eye stalks and the shorter receptors. I let open all pores on my skin to offer unfettered obeisance to my superior.

As my released pheromones made the rounds on the various officers' receptacles, I pondered over my predicament. Beside being physically and mentally exhausting _and_ a career trap, patrol training entailed a more than even chance to stop my police career, entirely.

Dying generally did that.

4

I OOZED IN FRONT of the large round Headquarters' entrance, under a maple tree whose root territory was invaded by alder brushes. The cabbage patch was a short distance from the burrows sheltering the plush GGPD offices.

The pinkish sky promised heat and sweat and tears. The sun was not even up, but the temperatures had risen to uncomfortable levels. The stupid ants crossed the field between the candidates gathering moisture and sustenance for the long trek ahead.

Training the recruits required getting them acquainted with all of the Greater Garden precinct, its temptations, its wonders and dangers. You couldn't do that from the comfortable burrow or the yummy cabbage patch. The candidates had to get the various olfactive landscapes of Garden down pat. They would have to keep a mental map of scents and areas and trees, to avoid the aster pods, to learn the proper method of crossing any exposed surface, and to understand when it was a good time to do so.

And they would have to affront their worst nightmares…

I extended my eyestalks and opened my receptors to get a good look at the current class.

There were seven sloggers.

I ran out the names in my head: one was missing.

The small two-cycle-old that had catapulted himself down and clogged everyone's nose with his triumphant scent call was not here. Wormshit, how I hated sloggers being late! That one would get a footload of acid from me as soon as he oozed in sight.

I concentrated on the others, ratting out ID scents.

The largest, Gol, had been the slowest in the race after Zgouish. He must have hatched at the very start of last cycle's spring, and found a lot to eat, to have reached his size.

The buddy next to his shell, Murr, had a narrow foot and the lean frame of a good messenger. He had also been in the race, behind…

Boon had mismatched eyestalks with a nervous twitch that made his visible signals difficult to decipher. Fortunately, his scent emissions were in proper working order.

Nool had a crack running diagonally across the spires of his orange and violet shell, which forced the police marker to etch the GGPD temp badge lower. The crack had not healed completely; a small triangular hole showed the glistening skin of his (normally covered) back. I averted my eyestalk, as it was an intimate region. I wondered briefly how he got such a mark, obviously a traumatic experience. Maybe he wouldn't make it to the end of the training, but you never knew.

The three others huddled close together, obviously afraid, and, if my sensors were accurate, obviously from the same clutch. They looked neither small nor big, your average, day-to-day slogger, except for the mottling of their foot, like permanent mud stains. There stalks moved almost in unison. They had so much in common that I dubbed them, in my head, the Trio.

I waited, but we would have to get going soon.

All in all, I thought, not a bad bunch. If they survived, they would be allowed to go on patrols with a partner and report crime. And I would make sure they survived.

I sucked moisture from the tender sprigs of grass, and prepared to address my small cohort. An abrupt emission of mating pheromones cut my careful planning. That release was quite impolite, or someone had not learned manners.

Yet.

I whirled, my lower foot sticking to the ground, only to find my late pupil innocently oozing his way toward the group. His shell looked even more oiled than the last day.

"Sorry," he signed out, "I got delayed at the first compost bin."

He said that while waving the rim of his foot in a dreaded 2–4 rhythm. The pace was too slow for an actual mating request, and he looked too intelligent not to know how out of place such a request would be at work. I surmised the new one was bragging about his recent prowess in the proverbial loose district of Comp-One.

Of course, I didn't act impressed, but the trio almost liquefied on their foot when they sniffed out the emission.

Time to get some discipline in this troop. I summoned my glands and sent a strong, acidic scent command.

"Get in line," I ordered. "Now!" I signed out.

The late candidate complied, languidly, like he didn't care, and joining the police was just a play. Like it was fun.

I would show this dim-witted braggart what a play it was!

"Where do you think you are, dunk-foot? On a cushy compost pile?"

I oozed, using the dew on the grass to augment my speed, passing all sloggers, and pushing back if necessary, until they made a wavy line. The braggart was the smallest of them, but he compensated by pushing pheromones all over the place! And two others were replying to the challenge and pumping hormones like water!

I looked up at the receding trunk of the maple whose roots encompassed the GGPD headquarters. If we stayed here, half of the stiffs working in the offices would be drawn out by the scented mating call.

And not only the stiffs. I smelled a familiar furry, milky sweat … as a shadow jumped over us, hind legs trailing gobs of earth.

DOWN! I broadcast, already contracting my body to get inside my shell. I felt a shock, as another of those rabbits sent me spinning sideways. As my shell came to rest, I felt the powerful vibration of another of those beasts bearing down on the ground.

From my shell aperture. I had a glimpse of them bouncing away, the long appendages of their vibration captors flapping on their back. They disappeared into the bushes lining the eastern Garden limit, into the neighboring precinct.

"Wha-wha-what was that?" Boon signaled, his unpaired stalks waving out of synch.

"Stompers," signed another, as I hefted my shell upright.

"I thought they were all dead," sent Nool, one eyes-talk peering from his shell's hole.

There had been a large family of rabbits living under the maple roots this spring, the cubs happily hopping everywhere and disturbing normal police operations. Eventually, predation and various accidents had prevailed over the stupidest of the young, which was usually most of them. We had a calm period before this active couple brought up a new litter into the world, disrupting the tranquility of the GGPD headquarters.

The Chief still regretted the death of Big Thumper. The burrows' previous occupant had been, to his saying, "a true gentle rabbit."

"Why do you put up with those mammals?" Big Gol asked, getting out of this upset shell.

There were several advantages to have those fast, loose and idiot rabbits around the GGPD headquarters. First, they scared off the smaller predators that usually preyed on law-abiding citizens. No snake tried to slither inside the burrow to get stomped upon by an excited cub, no winged death claws could dart under the branches without the rabbits tapping the ground, sending a vibration to the sloggers.

I gave the executive summary for the class.

"They contribute to the informal headquarters protection."

The small braggart sucked air through the pneumostome hole to expel some snide comment. His mere presence had become irritating. Not even Zgouish would put up with the youngling's arrogance. No way I would let him vent his air while we were already late for departure. I summoned my best authority phero-mones to push a stern command.

"Follow me!"

I heaved my shell in a no-nonsense move and set off down the path that followed the large stone slabs the giants used for going about. My first mission was to guide them around the full Garden perimeter, which would take three full days and nights. I had computed the best moisture shelters along the way.

After a few heartbeats, I felt that I was sliming alone. No one was following my trail.

I sniffed the air. A cloud of confusion was coming from the class. The braggart had released his comment (*why did they put us under a mere egg sack?*) and, not content to belittle a superior, was waving his sides in a suggestive pattern on a rhythm I didn't care to count. Problem was, his scent emission had not only come across my own order, but had dispelled and *superceded* it. Moreover, his love pheromones were washing all over the place.

Major dung.

This was not, I repeat, *not* helping at all to assert my authority.

That small clean-shelled candidate had the poten-tial to be a major career threat. Someone must have put him there to make me look bad. The candidate didn't look at all like police material with his small size and attitude. But oh, did he have the strongest emitting glands I had ever smelled! If I hadn't been a trained officer, I would have fallen head over foot to his mating dance.

Like others did.

The candidates' line had broken in wobbling units. Nool and Boon were sliming in the direction of the burrow. It was clear from his fluttering stalks that poor Boon had misplaced the origin of the mating call was intent on answering a mating call coming from the labs. Nool was hurrying after him.

Meanwhile, the Trio was oozing and oohing toward the braggart, and falling upon each other in doing so. Gol had not moved at all. He was placidly munching on a lettuce leave.

I had to plant my foot firmly over this group. I wish I had my partner's powerful glands to get my order across. I had to do something, fast, before the rest of my authority crumbled to nothing.

I oozed around the Trio, now rolling over in a tangled heap, slapping a shell in passing. I raised my head in the usual mating pattern imitated by the braggart. He rose to the challenge, of course, or, given his size, tried to. I resolved to a ruse that had served me before.

As he was revealing his genital aperture from which his love dart would point, I sent an answer totally at odds with my body language.

"So, you think you'll have it easy with an egg sack, won't you?"

That confused the braggart, his eyestalks retracting along with his dart. Before he could form a clever rejoinder, I hurled my foot down, sliming over his head and stalks with glee. This move clogged his pneumostome and did a good mucus job on his back. I had learned it from watching Zgouish proceed to unsavory arrests.

I only relented when I sensed the slogger retracting inside his tiny shell. A foamy mucus bubbled from his underside, a sure sign of the disturbance and aggravation he had just endured.

By the time I oozed back on the path, the six remaining candidates followed me, heads bowed, receptor stalks to the attention. From my experience, I guessed we would be a good distance down the path before the braggart came out from under his shell, but the slime trail shining behind us would be easy to follow, by sight or by scent.

If he decided police work was still for him.

5

THE RISING SUN chased away the grays of the dawn sky, turning it a soft pink. An incredible array of vivid colors flooded the Garden around us, lighting up the Back Door Area. The ball of fire was still too low on the horizon to be annoying. I expected to have a good part of the training done by the time we would need to shelter from its unforgiving rays.

Despite the initial annoyance, we had made good time, following the line of pale flat stones. We stayed close to the bottom of the slabs, our shells sometimes grating against the white wall. Some citizens resented the giants' existence, their furry predators and the rolling black deaths of the North Canyon, but their flat stones had saved countless Garden citizens from being trampled to death.

Of course, we were not the only ones appreciating the rewards of civilization. Red-torso ants lined up in the other direction, head to tail. I spotted a gray mouse, sitting still on the clump of grass sprouting from a neglected pass between two slabs. Beetles were busy preparing mud cakes for their eggs. At the intersections of slab paths, the mess of scents made a confusing puzzle.

Most of the Garden inhabitants moved faster than us, but, as the Chief liked to remind the impatient among us, few lived longer than we did. These ants careening along would never see the next spring.

The candidates oohed and aahed, stalks spinning in excitement. Most of them had never traveled past the composter bins sitting along the wood barrier. They were surprised to see that the barrier marking the jurisdiction's eastern limit continued, weed climbing on the smooth vertical planks. I could smell the paint on the surface.

"Do we have to hurry all day?" Gol inquired, munching on a grass blade.

He was the last in the line, behind the "initial annoyance" who had, mercifully, stayed quiet since he joined the back tail of our line. Brag's skin still exhaled undisciplined pheromones, but he had refrained from emitting any complaints or comments.

I stopped as we skirted the main viewing spot of Back Door Area. I cast about for the guard's scent signature. Guards were posted at the busiest times of the season, in spring when the new freshly hatched citizens tended to explore their neighborhood. As spring had glided into summer, only one lone stiff remained on the site, to warn off the slowest or the distracted.

I sensed no one. I sent a command signal that got no answer, except from some stupid red ants waving the hair-thin sensor antennas in wonder. Wasn't talking to you, buds.

Murr, the second in line, bumped against my shell.

"Why are we stopping?" he signed. Behind him, other shells had slowed down to a stop.

"A pause, for your education," I signed. "Don't move until I say so."

The guard was usually a five or six-cycle-old veteran, close to retirement. BDA shifts were usually given as a juicy reward, because the food there was stupendous. Of course, there was a catch, but each officer had been severely warned against the danger.

My sight was as low as any gastropod, but I used Zgouish's trick to peer at the forbidden territory. I strained both eyestalks as parallel as I could to check for the missing guard.

A riot of flowers in pots flanked the Back Door, near the big blue box full of metal and plastic containers. Higher up, the globe-shaped nest was still hanging under the gables, a few wasps buzzing around. I wondered about the informant queen. Maybe she used messengers.

New pots had been added in a row, their round, smooth flanks barely scratched. The giants must have kept those delicate plants indoor and waited for the heat to get them out. I recognized the wonderful taste of tomatoes, the fruits still small and acid, and the fresh green lances of chives, appetizing.

I looked up for a big, discolored five-cycle-old shell feasting on a pot of fragrant herbs. Eating on the job was allowed in the police, especially on long shifts, but failing to present oneself when a superior officer called wasn't. A hairy scent alarmed me. I twisted my neck toward the giant's set of white plastic chairs.

A motionless gray and black furred deathclaw was sprawled on one chair. This... *cat* (the Chief had taken upon himself to teach more vocabulary to his subordinates) was most probably resting from its quite active predation night. I drew upon the mucus reserves stored under my shell. A GGPD officer had few resources against predators, but attack mucus had served me well in the past.

All in all, I doubted the beast would budge for a small, hard-shelled, slimy prey.

Flies buzzed around, forming a low cloud over the ground. I opened my receptors to their widest, and immediately caught the sickly-sweet taste of the beer trap.

I sent another call, drawing from my moisture reserves.

It would reflect badly on the guard's rap sheet. I needed him to guide us near the trap, so I could explain the danger to the recruits, but not too close, so I did not lose pupils to the sweet fermented temptation. I sent a stern warning to my own troop to stick in place.

Scents of glue wafted out as Gol had taken the order literally. The quantity and quality of his production guaranteed no predator's beak or teeth could tear him from the ground.

I oozed on, keeping a low profile by skirting the flat ceramic tiles composing most of BDA's ground.

Those tiles were extra-smooth, shining as if the dew had permanently set on them. The enticing food smells forced me to contract my receptors. I would do nothing to gorge myself in front of the waiting recruits.

Contracting my receptors lowered the temptation offered by the tender leaves, but the cloying smell of the beer had a way of insisting. It was on my left, past the tiles, attended by several lines of ants. The beer pond was in fact (as I had learned) a plastic container placed inside a hole so the rim would be level with the surrounding ground.

Worker ants gobbled up a small quantity, stashed it in their second social stomach, and left. Some had felled into the hole, but not all. I glimpsed two ants and one yellow-and-black wasp, floating up.

Well, I was an officer and a gentle slogger: I knew better…

The beer was a mind as well as a physical trap. It was like a pernicious emission in the backyard of my brain: *You're strong, you do not need the precautions for the weak-minded, you can ooze closer to the rim, just a little closer…*

A waft of air on my skin alerted me. A dark death claw had alighted on the rim, and proceeded to peck ghoulishly at the beer, golden drops going down its beak.

The proximity of those three-pronged claws jolted me out of the trance. I regained my senses, less than one body length from the rim. I contracted my head and foot to disappear inside my shell, keeping one eyestalk up.

The bird (if I remembered the Chief's word for it) took no notice of a slogger across the wide circle of liquid death. Its wings batted the air, scattering several dots about, parasites. It flopped around more, trying to get at something under the surface.

Then it flew away. I cautiously unrolled from my shell.

Peering down the murky liquid under the dead wasp, I noticed the curve of a shell. The GGPD badge was visible on the largest spire.

6

CLOSING MY PNEUMOSTOME, I stuck my foot firmly in place. Then, I extended my body until it gained twice its previous length, so my eyestalks hung over the brown liquid. There was no error about the badge.

The officer's body had partially rotated so his limp stalks jutted out from the shell's curve.

Having just experienced the powerful attraction of the trap, I could not find in my heart the will to blame the poor about-to-retire guard.

Maybe he had been ill, or unable to mate, and had decided to end his life then and there. I pulled in my stalks and started a half-turn, oozing mucus to dissolve the glue. Time to get back to my waiting class.

Except that they were cluttering the space right behind me. While I was pondering over the drowned officer, Gol and the others had left the path and followed my slime trail.

The braggart, being the fastest, had taken the head. For an anguishing moment, I envisioned his pushing me over the rim.

With his slighter mass, he couldn't muscle me over, but he had stuck his foot down. It would be a battle of adherence until the weakest one got unstuck.

Then the thought left me because Brag's eyestalks waved in the direction of the drowned shell.

"Was he the one that was supposed to guide us?" he emitted.

This time he had kept his pheromones levels low. I sent a short agreement puff, trying my best not to sniff the tantalizing beer.

"There's another one," Gol said.

He had moved his ginormous shell (was he only two cycles old?) on another quadrant of the beer pond. With his appetite, Gol was a catastrophe waiting to happen.

Stand back! I emitted, acidic fear lacing my words.

I could have talked to a wall. Gol didn't budge, extending his head over the murky pond like I did before.

"There's another one," he repeated. I moved sideways toward him and looked. A small yellow ball bumped softly against the big shell.

The scenario of the guard's death reformed in my head. A young, freshly hatched, had somehow passed through the perimeter and fallen into the deadly pool. The old gentleslogger had valiantly plunged to rescue the hatchling. That he failed to save the little one didn't surprise me. Before we put guards around, entire clutches could be lost, like Zgouish's bros.

Swimming in the thick liquid was impossible with a heavy shell. He must have known it, though.

Why did he try?

An acrid tang, stronger than the beer smell all around us, reached me.

"It moved!" the braggart screamed, his olfactive call unmistakable. That one, if he survived and dropped his badass attitude, would make a good commander some day.

I extended my body, again. Yes, tiny stalks were moving about, in a desperate attempt to … climb the shell. This must have been the dead officer's idea when he plunged to his death!

If the young slogger had been on the ground, it could have secreted glue. Alas, its small foot awash in beer, the hatchling was getting no purchase on the bigger shell.

"Awww, poor baby!" the Trio exclaimed, eye stalks signing in common sorrow.

"Nothing to do, unless you want to dry," Boon uttered, his mismatched stalks garbling his meaning.

"Looks yummy," Gol said, his mouth watering.

"It's sad what those giants do," signed Nool.

I relaxed my eyestalks. Despite the sadness of the occasion, this was as good a time to drive home the lesson.

"This is why Back Door Area is a mortal place," I signed. "Beer is a powerful addictive. Don't absorb a drop of it. Don't let anyone come inside the perimeter."

I let the lesson sink, then added, releasing my most convincing scent: "Now, scoot!"

A ripple crossed the smooth surface of the pond. Shocked, I tensed my stalks again, then recoiled in horror.

Ignoring my fresh order, the stupidest of the class, AKA the Trio, were splashing about into the trap!

"Shit worm! What are you doing—"

I stopped because my pungent warning did not cross the beer barrier. Two members of the Trio had already disappeared under the surface.

Wormshit. The temptation had been too compelling. Losing two candidates so soon in the training tour would not reflect well on me. And big Gol was cheering on, as if his comrades' deaths meant nothing to him.

Then I noticed, or rather smelled, the last member of the Trio. Third had not followed his bros into the beer.

Instead, he had secreted enough glue under his mottled foot to stick to the plastic rim. Its body had extended to its full length, its serrated teeth grabbing the foot end of Second, who was, as I peered down the dark pool, biting the tail of the first who had plunged.

The beer was too thick to see the moves under it, but more ripples crossed and re-cross the surface. I wanted to avert my stalks, because when you fell under the liquid, you didn't drown immediately. It could take minutes before the pneumostome was clogged by liquid, and more minutes before the lungs gave up, then the brain, quarter by quarter. So Zgouish, having survived the trap by sheer luck, told me.

The death throes of First and Second sent more high-frequency ripples to the rim.

Meanwhile, Gol had stuck his enormous foot on the rim, next to Third, and was happily gurgling beer. Dung. I was about to lose three of them. Maybe even four, because Third would be a mental mess afterward. No wonder he was holding so fast on his clutch bros.

Brag had set himself on the other side of Third, his stalks spinning madly, signing encouragement. That's when I noticed that Gol had, in fact, clamped his wide, wide mouth on a free portion of Second's tail and was pulling with all his might, helping Third.

Second was finally lifted from the beer. Gol twisted and deposited his fellow candidate nearby. By this time, Third had released Second's tail and seized First's. This time, Braggart helped, his small mouth biting hard on First's tail, his skin exuding boasting and reassurance in powerful bursts.

The slogger's flanks were rippling as the last member of the Trio was pulled out.

As Brag oozed sideways while he was pulling (no slogger, except the best trained officers, could *back up* on his slime trail), more of First's mottled body emerged, more and more, until … a glistening yellow shape appeared!

Nool stepped in. He delicately seized the dripping hatchling in his mouth and twisted sideways to deposit him on the moist cement. Then he oozed clear mucus to wash the worst of the beer from the hatchling's breathing hole. For a horrible minute, I thought that we had been too late.

Then, the sides of the hatchling's foot trembled, and its stalks spun, groggy from the beer it has unwillingly ingested.

He was alive!

Proper hierarchy went off the drain: scented cheers erupted all around, enough to wake the gray and black striped deathclaw resting on the chair. The cat sniffed around. Its green eyes traveled over our party, then closed again as our slow moves did not provide much excitement.

7

ONCE WE HAD TRAILED SAFELY out of the zone with our rescued hatchling, there were tasks to attend to, a report to send.

First, warning GGPD Headquarters to appoint a new officer to guard the BDA perimeter.

Murr, the fastest slogger after Braggart, had immediately volunteered for the challenge. He assured us he would follow our slime trail and return in no time (meaning, in slogger's speech, before sundown).

Second, we had to get the small frightened one to a safe and moist haven.

Nool had offered himself for getting the youngling in a safe place. The hatchling was sticking with the candidate, its small stalk stroking the cracked shell. I guessed Nool's own traumatic experience had forged a bond with the young. I gave him the scented signature of a close-by shelter.

Before I sent them on, I considered the batch of sloggers lining in front of me.

Gol's head was oscillating, as he may have ingested some beer, but his mass and powerful glue had kept him from falling in.

At first, I had thought the Trio unworthy because how they swooned over the Braggart's heady pheromones. But in this dire situation, they had stuck together and, instead of drowning, had saved the hatchling. Their linking method would be added to our bag of tricks.

I thought about the lone guard and amended my report. I requested that Headquarters named at least _two_ near-retirement guards, so they could help each other if another accidental fall occurred.

As for Brag, once he managed to keep his emissions down (under my, ahem, firm suggestion), he had been mostly helping his classmates and providing strong encouragement.

Pride swelled under my shell.

As the sun's slanted rays bathed the group, I felt that this patrol training was shaping up better than I had anticipated.

The devious ME had been filled with glee, so happy to get me stuck with a bunch of less-than-promising candidates. Most of the older officers had given up on this batch and Zgouish, who genuinely cared for them, had been turned down. Even our lofty Chief had expressed reservations about them.

Well, they could eat worm dung!

Those recruits had the makings of fine officers that would, one day, be an asset for the Greater Garden Police Department.

THE END

Heartfelt Thanks

The first story of the GGPD, *Slime & Crime,*
has been originally published in Fiction River 22,
2017, edited by WMG Publishing inc. under the
direction of John Helfers.

If you enjoyed this story, share your impressions
on your favorite platform like Goodreads.com.
This way, you gently guide more readers towards
Michèle's stories.

Praise for Slime & Crime

"Laframboise does an excellent job of translating the rhythm and feel of the typical murder mystery into the realities of a snail's eye view. The story is clever and effectively conveys the point of view of the snails and the various limitations and talents available to them."

-- Robert Turner, Tangent

In the same series:

Greater Garden Snail Police - 1 Slime & Crime

Greater Garden Snail Police - 2 Back Door Area

Greater Garden Snail Police - 3 Green Snake

Greater Garden Snail Police - 4 A Gentleslogger Agreement (upcoming)

About the Author

WHEN NOT TRYING to initiate first contact with strange flora, Michèle Laframboise juggles her time between drawing comics and crafting stories.

A science-fiction lover since childhood, she has published 19 novels and more than 50 short stories, earning three Auroras and two Solaris awards.

Her works have appeared in *Solaris, Carmilla, Galaxies, Géante Rouge, Brin d'Éternité, Tesseracts, Fiction River, Compelling Science Fiction*, and *Abyss&Apex*. She has been translated into French, Italian and Russian.

Holding degrees in geography and engineering, Michèle uses her scientific background to create worlds filled with humor, invention and wonder.

Official website:
www.michele-laframboise.com
in French and English

Humoristic blog:
sundayartist.wordpress.com

Publisher's website:
www.echofictions.com

Wikipedia entry: Michèle Laframboise

For some news and amusing reading reviews, join
 Michele's happy band of readers!

http://michele-laframboise.com/fans

Other books by Michèle

Change or die!

Science-fiction / humor / First contact

Loongunis need constant fluctuations to thrive, while the strange-haired Earthmen hate the endless unstability.

When a sabotage impairs the shift engines of their traveling Box, the enforced immobility might drive all Loongunis mad...unless their translator can work out a solution!

Science fiction adventure at its best, a quirky 7000-word story told by multiple award-winning author Michèle Laframboise.

How to Think inside the Box
978-1-988339-40-5 (print)

Trapped in the most beautiful place on earth...

Humor / mystery / Ornithology

Equipped with her Sibley Guide and trusty binoculars, Amanda Byrd pursues the most elusive winged species. As she explores a beautiful canyon at dawn, Amanda discovers their lift sabotaged, trapping their group at the canyon's bottom.

Who did it, and why?

Our intrepid birdwatcher must find a way out before the sun turns the canyon into a mortal cauldron.

A short and spirited cozy mystery introducing the energetic Lady Byrd, written by Michèle Laframboise, multi-award winner author and amateur ornithologist.

Condor Cliff

ISBN 978-1-988339-08-5 (Print)

You won't forget Malak...

Child Labor/ Humanitarian / Sweatshops

Theo, a dispirited workplace humanitarian, audits a child worker at a cardboard factory, in a port city somewhere in Asia. He is impressed by young Malak's maturity and grit. When that boy, the same age as Theo's own son, disappears, he cannot let it rest. His quest for answers only raises more questions about the traps of structured help and acquired privilege.

An unsettling story quietly told by multiple awards-winning author Michèle Laframboise.

Cardboard Boy

ISBN 978-1-988339-22-1 (Print)

More on Echofictions.com/books

Friends' List

A story links every reader in a chain of friendship. Feel free to write your name before you give this book to someone close.

This is a unique feature of the printed edition!

Yearning for more Stories?

Michèle Laframboise's full bibliography is enough to whet any reader's appetite! Visit her author site at:
michele-laframboise.com

New stories are brewing up constantly!

To get exclusive offers, curated book reviews, advanced information on events, join Michele's happy band of readers!

michele-laframboise.com/fans

As a very busy writer, Michèle won't send mail more often than once every two months.